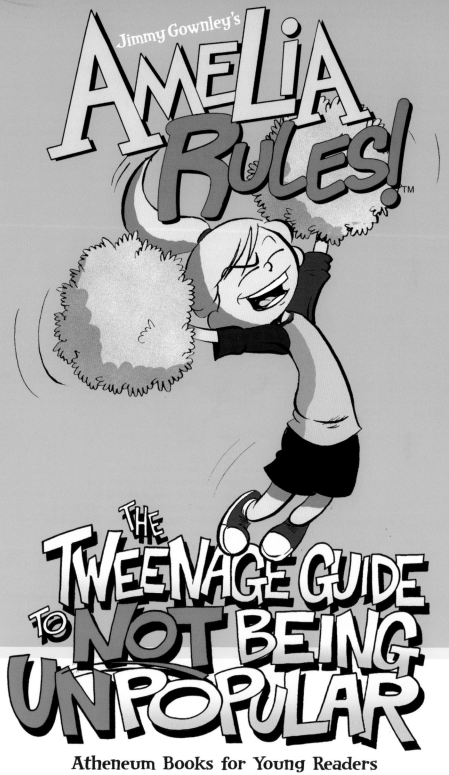

Jimmy Gownley's

AMELIA RULES!™

THE TWEENAGE GUIDE TO NOT BEING UNPOPULAR

Atheneum Books for Young Readers
New York London Toronto Sydney

This book is dedicated
with love and gratitude to
Michael Cohen, Harold Buchholz,
and Judy Hansen.

ATHENEUM BOOKS FOR YOUNG READERS
An imprint of Simon & Schuster Children's Publishing Division
1230 Avenue of the Americas, New York, New York 10020
This book is a work of fiction. Any references to historical events, real people,
or real locales are used fictitiously. Other names, characters, places, and incidents
are products of the author's imagination, and any resemblance to actual
events or locales or persons, living or dead, is entirely coincidental.
Copyright © 2010 by Jimmy Gownley
Atheneum Books for Young Readers is a registered trademark of Simon & Schuster, Inc.
For information about special discounts for bulk purchases, please contact Simon & Schuster Special Sales
at 1-866-506-1949 or business@simonandschuster.com.
The Simon & Schuster Speakers Bureau can bring authors to your live event.
For more information or to book an event, contact the Simon & Schuster Speakers Bureau
at 1-866-248-3049 or visit our website at www.simonspeakers.com.
Also available in an Atheneum Books for Young Readers hardcover edition
Book design by Sonia Chaghatzbanian
The text for this book is hand-lettered.
The illustrations for this book are digitally rendered.
Manufactured in the United States of America
0310 WOR
First Edition
2 4 6 8 10 9 7 5 3 1
CIP data for this book is available from the Library of Congress.
ISBN 978-1-4169-8610-2
ISBN 978-1-4169-8608-9 (pbk)

Don't Expect Miracles!

(A Note From the Author)

If you've purchased this book, I am sorry.

Sorry that you have had to live your life as an outsider, a nerd, a loser. Sorry that it took you so long to gain access to my wisdom.

But that's okay, because now we've found each other.

Within this book, you will find many helpful tips, exercises, and activities that will help you raise your social standing.

But, before we begin, a word of warning.

Don't expect miracles.

Most of you will never be popular. You will never be prom queens or kings. You will never be class president or voted most likely to, well, do anything positive.

But together, with hard work and dedication, we might be able to prevent you from embarrassing yourself any further.

So remember: Fate and genetics may have already decided that you will never be popular, but at least, with my help, you need no longer be UNpopular.

Dr. Victoria Medeochrias

Dr. Victoria Medeochrias

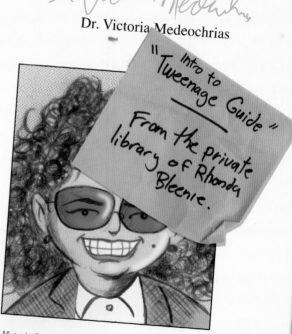

"Intro to Tweenage Guide"

From the private library of Rhonda Bleenie.

Victoria St. James Medeochrias is a world reknowned author, scholar, and motivational speaker. Her many books have been global bestsellers, and it is assumed that at least one of them helped someone, somewhere.

OKAY. I'M GONNA TELL YOU A STORY...

SEE, FIRST SOMETHING *BAD* HAPPENED.

HA HA HA HA HA HA

THEN THINGS GOT WORSE.

RUN!

I'M RUNNING.

OF COURSE THERE WAS SOME WEIRDNESS.

AAAAAAA

THE AMAZING MOBILE

BUT THEN SOMETHING AMAZING HAPPENED.

OR AT LEAST I THINK IT DID.

IT'S KINDA HARD KNOWING WHERE TO START.

SO, JUST FOR FUN, WE'LL START IN THE MIDDLE.

5

POPULARITY...

8

11

14

23

WHEN I GOT HOME, I WAS LUCKY TO FIND MOM AND TANNER WATCHING SOME WEEPY OLD MOVIE.

MOM (OF COURSE) WAS CRYING LIKE A *BABY*...

...WHILE TANNER (OF COURSE) WAS JUST LAUGHING HER *HEAD* OFF.

BUT BOTH OF THEM WERE INTO IT ENOUGH THAT NO ONE CARED WHETHER OR NOT I WENT TO BED *EARLY*.

LOOK, I KNOW YOU WANNA KNOW WHAT LANDED ME IN THAT *TREE*...

...BUT I JUST CAN'T TALK ABOUT IT YET.

BUT THAT NIGHT I SURE *THOUGHT* ABOUT IT.

YEAH.

I THOUGHT ABOUT IT A LOT.

29

MORE LIKELY, IT WOULD BE SOMETHING A LITTLE MORE SOPHISTICATED...
INVOLVING...SAY, *PHOTOSHOP*, AND A WELL-PLACED *RUMOR*.

OUR NUMBER TWO STORY TONIGHT: A FALL FROM GRACE SO SPECTACULAR, MILTON HIMSELF COULD SCARCELY HAVE IMAGINED IT...

...AS OCCASIONALLY BELOVED TWEEN-QUEEN AMELIA LOUISE McBRIDE PLUMMETS FROM THE HEIGHTS OF ROLE-MODEL HEAVEN, INTO THE DEPTHS OF TABLOID HECK.

2 NOT PICKING A WINNER
top stories

TODAY, LEAKED PHOTOS SHOW McBRIDE IN A VARIETY OF UNSAVORY SITUATIONS, INCLUDING, BUT NOT LIMITED TO, ATTENDING A RALLY FOR PEOPLE AGAINST BABIES...

...AND PARTYING AT THE VIPER ROOM WITH PARIS HILTON AND SOMEONE WHO MAY, OR MAY NOT, BE LORD VOLDEMORT.

DIAPERS STINK!

DON'T "RATTLE" ME!

DROOL AIN'T COOL!!

2 TWEEN MOB
top stories

2 AMELIA McFRIED
top stories

REALLY, ALL I COULD DO WAS PREPARE FOR THE WORST.

BUT THERE WAS ONE THING I COULDN'T PREPARE FOR...

...AND THAT THING... WAS NOTHING.

SEE, THEY DIDN'T *HAVE* TO DO SOMETHING TO ME. NOT WHEN JUST *IGNORING* ME WORKED SO MUCH *BETTER*.

AND ONCE I GOT THE POINT... ONCE I KNEW WHAT WAS GOING ON...

...THEN THEY COULD GO TO WORK.

FIRST, REGGIE AND PAJAMAMAN GOT PEELED AWAY. SOME GUYS WERE ASKING REGGIE DUMB TRIVIA QUESTIONS ABOUT, LIKE, THE FANTASTIC FOUR, AND, OF COURSE, REGGIE ATE IT UP WITH A BIG GEEK SPOON.

NO, NO.

DOCTOR DOOM IS IN #5!

AND HE WAS GONE.

THEN THESE GIRLS GRABBED RHONDA AND STARTED CHATTING HER EAR OFF. I NEVER EVEN SAW THEM *LOOK* AT HER BEFORE.

AND SOME OF THE GIRLS WERE... WHAT, *SIXTH GRADERS?* I DIDN'T EVEN KNOW THEIR NAMES, Y'KNOW?

THEN *SHE* WAS GONE.

AND I WAS ALONE.

SUDDENLY I FELT LIKE I DIDN'T KNOW *ANY* ONE... OR ANYTHING.

BUMP

SOCIAL STUDIES

36

38

39

43

45

47

49

51

BRITNEY WAS ON A ROLL. SHE WAS MERCILESS. AND RHONDA? WELL, SHE JUST STOOD THERE, *TAKING IT.*

AS FOR ME, WELL...

...ALL I COULD THINK OF WAS MY LOCKER.

MY HEART SANK.

THE SAME PINEAPPLE PIZZA THAT RHONDA BOUGHT JUST CUZ SHE KNEW I LIKED IT. YET THERE I WAS, LETTING HER BE INSULTED.

AND THEN, SOMEWHERE DEEP INSIDE MY BRAIN...

...SOMETHING WENT...

BECAUSE IN MY LOCKER WAS MY *LUNCH BAG.*

MATH

AMELIA

...WERE LEFTOVER SLICES OF *PINEAPPLE PIZZA....*

AND...

IN MY *LUNCH BAG...*

55

SLAM

"BAD"?

Hmm...

I AM *NOT* BAD!

AM I?

I MEAN, I DON'T *FEEL* BAD.

OF COURSE, I DON'T FEEL PARTICULARLY *GOOD,* EITHER.

MAYBE IF YOU'RE BAD, YOU'RE THE LAST ONE TO KNOW, Y'KNOW?

I BET MOST BAD PEOPLE WHO DO BAD THINGS DON'T EVEN THINK THEY'RE BAD, OR THINK THE BAD THINGS THEY DO ARE BAD, AND THAT'S JUST TOO BAD...

I THINK.

64

OOOKEY-DOKEY!

I'LL SEE WHAT I CAN DO.

NOW, FRANKENSTEIN...

* ACTUALLY, I'M NOT FRANKENSTEIN. I'M FRANKENSTEIN'S MONSTER

SORRY, MY BAD!

THAT MUST BE REALLY ANNOYING.

* WELL, HEH-HEH, I ADMIT IT CAN BE QUITE VEXING AT TIMES.

I'M SURE.

NOW, MR MONSTER, WHAT DO YOU HAVE TO SAY FOR YOURSELF...

ARE YOU BAD?

*YOU'RE SPEAKING OF A MORE HIGHLY DEVELOPED MORALITY THAN I AM CAPABLE OF UNDERSTANDING. YOU SEE, TO ME, "BAD" IMPLIES A STATE OF THREAT, OF PERIL, IF YOU WILL, RATHER THAN A (ARGUABLY, I'LL GRANT YOU) MORE SUBJECTIVE STATE OF BEING.

OH, I SEE. THEN CAN YOU GIVE ME AN EXAMPLE OF "BAD," AS YOU UNDERSTAND IT?

* HMM...

OKAY, NOW I KNOW THAT WHETHER, OR NOT I'M *BAD*, I CAN SOMETIMES BE A LITTLE, Y'KNOW... TOUGH TO TAKE.

AND WHAT YOU'RE ABOUT TO SEE WILL PROBABLY IMPROVE MY IMAGE.

Juliana Hatfield vs. Dr. Bones McCoy

Mom, Aunt Tanner, I have bad news.

BUT ON THE **OTHER** HAND....

AWWWWWWW HE SAID "MOMMY"!

HEY!

SO, TO SUM UP...

...WE REPRESENT A SEMI-FLEXIBLE, LUMPY-HAIRED, SMART MOUTH WITH NO CATCH PHRASE.

AND THAT'S... COMBINED.

HMM...

MAYBE WE SHOULD MOVE TO PHASE TWO.

GOOD IDEA.

SO...

WHAT'S PHASE TWO?

PHASE TWO:

MAKEOVERS!

Face it. We live in a country where 83% of all citizens are obese and the other 17% have eating disorders. Now, I know I just made those statistics up, but that doesn't change the fact that unless you're 60% plastic, there's probably something wrong with the way you look.

Many people misunderstand the point of makeovers. Makeovers are not about making you look good, they are about making you look trendy. Also, they are about making you appear to be something you are not. This works to your advantage, though, as what you are must not be much, or you wouldn't be reading this book.

If you're still at a loss for where to start, my rule of thumb is to dress and act as age inappropriate as possible. The chart below should prove to be a useful makeover guide for the rest of your soon-to-be trend-obsessed life.

Ages 12–16—Dress like an 18–25-year-old, act like a 25–30-year-old.

Ages 17–21—Dress like a 25–30-year-old, act like a 12-year-old.

Ages 22–30—Dress like a 16-year-old, act like an old Madonna song.

Ages 31–45—Dress like a 50-year-old, read your old yearbook a lot.

Ages 46–up—Just try to stay indoors as much as possible.

Dr. V. - On the Record

(cont. from p. 23)

book has been very controversial, especially among—
A: Opinionated loudmouths. (*laughs*)

Q: I was going to say "educators." How do you answer the charges that your book reinforces negative attitudes among children?
A: Well, those people have a right to be wrong (*laughs*), you know? (*sighs*) The way I see it, I'm just being realistic. People just don't enjoy hearing the truth. It makes them feel uncomfortable.

Q: And your book is the truth?
A: Absolutely. See, the problem is parents spend so much time telling their kids that they're special, right? That they can do anything. But that's not true. That's why very few parents encourage their kid to excel once the child is out of school.

Q: What do you mean?
A: Well, when a child is coming up through the ranks in school, he or she is encouraged to do well, to distinguish him- or herself, to strive for excellence. But as soon as he or she get a diploma and a degree, what do people tell them then? "Get a job with benefits, keep your head down, and wait to die."

Q: That's grim.
A: But it's true.

Q: So you say striving for excellence should be a life-long process?
A: (*laughs*) No, no. Just the opposite. My book is about dispelling the notions that each child is special. Most children are average by definition. Of course, do what you can to improve your standing, but be realistic. Accept your place in the pecking order early, and you'll have a lot less disappointment later in life. Don't expect miracles.

Q: And you think this is good advice?
A: My book has sold four million copies.

Did You Know?

1. Dr. V.'s books are translated into more than fourteen languages, including, French, Italian, Swahili, and Gullah.

2. When practicing for her driver's exam, the young Ms. V. ran over her own foot while practicing a three-point turn.

3. In high school she was voted student body president. Her first act was to disband the pep squad.

4. She has a twin brother. The two have not spoken in eleven years. This is due to what family insiders refer to as "hatred."

Recent Interview with "Guide" Author "Dr. V."

SO, YEAH. I WAS GROUNDED FOR A WEEK. I'D LIKE TO SAY I SPENT THE TIME, Y'KNOW, STUDYING OR READING OR LEARNING TO JUGGLE OR SOMETHING.

BUT MOSTLY, I JUST READ MY COPY OF THE TWEENAGE GUIDE.

THERE ARE PROBABLY WORSE WAYS TO SPEND YOUR TIME, BUT I CAN'T THINK OF ANY RIGHT NOW.

A TWEENAGE GUIDE
CASE STUDY:
The Princess Effect

You can learn a lot from Snow White. Whether in the original Grimm's fairy tale, or any of the later theatrical versions, this chick is a great example of upwardly mobile social climbing! And hey, you can apply some of her techniques to your own life. But avoid the traps that the evil queen represents! Let's compare and contrast below.

SNOW WHITE

(1) Social Climbing
Scullery maid to princess with only a bad case of indigestion in between!

(2) Flexibility
Lose your spot at the castle? Slum it at the dwarfs'. Then ditch 'em when Mr. Right shows up.

(3) Ignorance Is Bliss
Other than pie making, knowing stuff doesn't seem to be one of SW's strengths. But who cares? She still wins.

EVIL QUEEN

(1) Knowledge
She knows chemistry, botany, and it appears a great deal more. What good did it do her?

(2) That Dumb Mirror
If you have something bad to say, save it for the Internet.

(3) Bad Makeover
Beauty queen to hag? No wonder she gets killed by an angry mob!

Who are your dwarfs? Is there a group on the next level up you can use for the time being? For example, if you're in the AV club, upgrade to the chess club, but be prepared to ditch them if the cheerleaders call.

Are you Prince Ready? Remember the lessons of our makeover chapter. Snow White always looked her best, even when she was dead. The least you can do is wear a nice skirt to school.

Can you bake a pie? It's always nice to have at least one semi-useful skill. Pick something fairly easy, but with a high show-off factor.

ANYWAY...

Getting Desperate

Look, if you've read this far and are still not seeing the results you desire, there can be two possibilities:

(1) You may be like Aunt Edna's noodles. More on that in the next chapter, but be aware that it's not good.

(2) You may just need a little extra attention. If you think this second option applies to you, then why not drop me a line?

Write to me, care of the address in the front of this book; a real letter now, not an e-mail, and there is a chance I'll write back with custom advice relating to your specific needs. I mean, there's not a good chance, but what the heck, it's not like you have anything else to do, right?

this second

Write to me,
etter now, n
with custom
here's not a

Dear Dr. V.,

I'm not really
sure why
I'm writing
to you.

I mean, it's not like I'm one of those
"unpopular" kids that need your book.
Pretty much everyone likes me! I mean,
why wouldn't they?

HMM...

CRINKLE
CRINKLE

THUNK

"I LOVE YOU ANYWAY."

THE PHRASE JUST POPPED IN MY HEAD, Y'KNOW?

BELIEVE ME, *LOVE* WAS THE *LAST* THING I WAS FEELING.

BUT IT FELT TRUE SOMEHOW....

BETTER THAN TRUE...

IT FELT *GOOD!*

I LET IT ROLL OVER AND OVER AGAIN IN MY MIND.

"I LOVE YOU ANYWAY."

"I LOVE YOU ANYWAY."

140

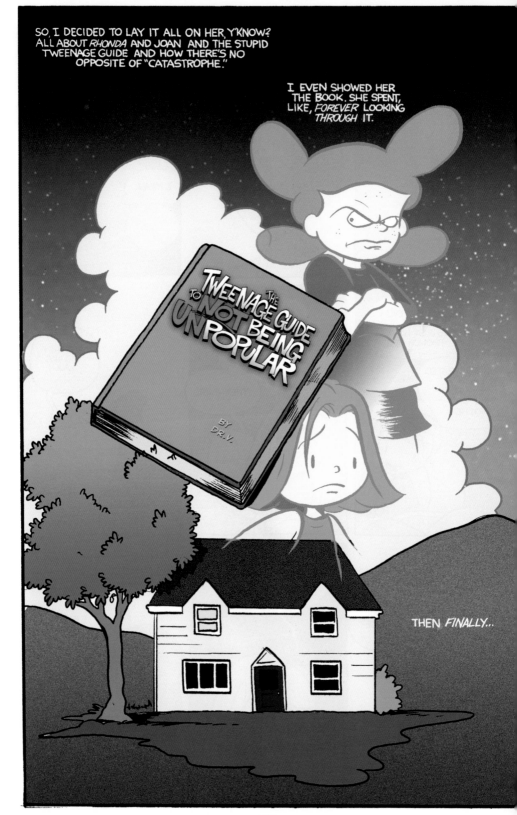

SO, I DECIDED TO LAY IT ALL ON HER, Y'KNOW? ALL ABOUT *RHONDA* AND JOAN AND THE STUPID *TWEENAGE GUIDE* AND HOW THERE'S NO OPPOSITE OF "CATASTROPHE."

I EVEN SHOWED HER THE BOOK. SHE SPENT, LIKE, *FOREVER* LOOKING *THROUGH* IT.

THE TWEENAGE GUIDE TO NOT BEING UNPOPULAR

BY DR. V.

THEN *FINALLY*...

143

149

155

I COULDN'T BELIEVE IT! I COULDN'T BELIEVE I MADE IT, AND I COULDN'T BELIEVE HOW *EXCITED* IT MADE ME!

AND I COULDN'T HELP BUT *WONDER* HOW EVERYONE WOULD REACT.

I'LL BET IT WILL BLOW REGGIE'S MIND! I THOUGHT...

AND KYLE... WELL... HE'LL INSULT ME, BUT, HE'LL DIG IT... OH, YEAH... HE'LL DIG IT!

TANNER WILL *LAUGH*, BUT SHE'LL SECRETLY BE *PROUD*.

MOM TOO....

AND RHONDA WILL...

RHONDA WILL HATE ME.

AGAIN!

159

FOR A MINUTE, AFTER I WOKE UP, I SORTA *FORGOT* ABOUT EVERYTHING. MAYBE IT WAS CUZ I SLEPT ON THE COUCH, BUT EVERYTHING SEEMED KINDA *DIFFERENT.*

BUT THAT WAS ONLY FOR A MINUTE, Y'KNOW? ONCE I GOT MY BEARINGS, I DECIDED, OKAY...

...I'LL GET DRESSED, AND GO TO SCHOOL, AND RHONDA WON'T MAKE THE TEAM, AND THEN SHE'LL HATE ME BECAUSE I *DID,* AND THEN EVERYTHING WILL BE ALL *CRAPPY* AGAIN.

TURNIP BRAIN DOESN'T GET IT, NO MATTER HOW MANY TIMES HE PULLS ON THAT DUMB DOOR, IT'S *NEVER* GONNA OPEN! IT'S JUST LIKE MY *LIFE*... Y'KNOW?

I MEAN, I'VE WOKEN UP, AND GONE TO SCHOOL *ZILLIONS* OF TIMES, AND IT'S ALWAYS THE *SAME*...A *CATASTROPHE!* AND LIKE DR. V. SAYS ...

161

BUT SUDDENLY...

THERE IT WAS...

...THE OPPOSITE
OF
CATASTROPHE...

SNOW WHITE..

166

169

175

THINKING ABOUT IT, I'M NOT REALLY SURE *WHY* I GAVE UP MY SPOT FOR RHONDA.

I GUESS IT WAS PARTLY BECAUSE I KNEW WHAT IT WOULD MEAN TO HER.

CONC LUS ION

I hope that this

helpful to you. E

ugh

have

AND, PARTLY, I GUESS IT WAS LIKE *TANNER* SAID... IT FELT *RIGHT.*

IT FELT *GOOD.*

obably not, but we c

think that you co

any

out I was mo

that's what it

BUT BETWEEN YOU AND ME? IT WAS ALSO BECAUSE HAVING THE SPOT AND TURNING IT *DOWN* WAS EVEN *COOLER* THAN ACTUALLY BEING ON THE SQUAD, *Y'KNOW?*

uld n

e? I didn't

are at parents' money. After all,

EVEN IF I *WAS* THE ONLY ONE WHO *KNEW* ABOUT IT.

pe you a t least

n being a compl

be you a t

e you ven hou

ould you

e? Did yo

her th

h

 u

e and

lete and

I DON'T KNOW, MAYBE THAT DOESN'T EVEN MAKE ANY *SENSE....*

that will help you from

ok has been

a horrible wretch,

n't w

ging o

re than

's all abou

u ever really

an what you

appy to take your

you a

obvious

found

tip o

utte

DRAW YOUR OWN CONCLUSIONS, I GUESS.

l hope, ca

ALL I KNEW WAS THAT THE DECISION WAS *MADE.*

183